CHANGES

written and illustrated by
TRAVIS WILLIAMS

LANDMARK EDITIONS, INC.
P.O. Box 4469 • 1402 Kansas Avenue • Kansas City, Missouri 64127

Dedicated to:
Crawford Killian,
who helped get me started;
and to my mom who knows why.

Many thanks to the models
for my illustrations:
Ray Williams, Diane Williams,
Bryn Williams, Art Reiber,
Bob Patterson, Joene Hawk,
Dave Sept, Jim Lochhead,
and Dustin Pickout

COPYRIGHT © 1993 TRAVIS WILLIAMS

International Standard Book Number: 0-933849-44-3 (LIB.BDG.)

Library of Congress Cataloging-in-Publication Data
Williams, Travis, 1975-
    Changes / written and illustrated by Travis Williams.
    p.   cm.
    Summary: When thirteen-year-old Jay Brady tries to find out what has happened to a classmate who has disappeared, he encounters increasingly strange and frightening occurrences.
    ISBN 0-933849-44-3 (lib.bdg. : acid-free paper)
    [1. Science fiction.]

I. Title.
PZ7.W66828Ch   1993
[Fic]—dc20
                                    93-13420
                                    CIP
                                    AC

Editorial Coordinator: Nancy R. Thatch
Creative Coordinator: David Melton

Printed in the United States of America

Landmark Editions, Inc.
P.O. Box 4469
1402 Kansas Avenue
Kansas City, Missouri 64127
(816) 241-4919

CHANGES

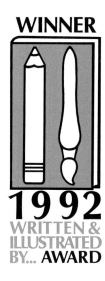

Landmark initiated THE NATIONAL WRITTEN & ILLUS-TRATED BY...AWARDS CONTEST FOR STUDENTS, so young people in the United States would have the opportunity to become published authors and illustrators. But when a number of Canadian teachers and librarians heard about our contest, they also began to encourage their students to develop original books and enter them in the competition.

Since we had nothing against Canadian students, we welcomed their entries in the same spirit as we accepted the works created by American students. And because many of the Canadian entries were so good, our editors began to suspect that we would soon have a Canadian winner.

They were right; that very thing has happened! In the upper age category of the 1992 Contest, the book CHANGES, written and illustrated by Travis Williams, from Sardis, British Columbia, was selected as the First Place Winner. When you read Travis's extraordinary book, you will understand why our judges were so impressed with his skills as a writer and his talents as an illustrator.

In his gripping narrative, Travis offers a slice of science fiction that is laced with the elements of a top-notch mystery. Something strange is happening to the students who attend a middle school. One by one, they are disappearing, and after they are gone, they are quickly forgotten by their families and friends. Only one teen-age boy tries to find out what is happening to his classmates. By doing so, he soon discovers that he has placed his own life in jeopardy.

The reader will find nothing common or ordinary about Travis's skills as a storyteller. He knows where to place the chills and how to pace the thrills in his text. Scene by scene and step by step, he tightens the net of suspense as he weaves a sinister web of intrigue. And his pencil illustrations have a stark, dark edge that add shadowed realism to the unfolding mystery.

I now offer you a remarkable reading experience. All you have to do is turn the page and enter a place where changes are about to begin.

— David Melton
Creative Coordinator
Landmark Editions, Inc.

I didn't hear the woman come up behind me, so I was startled when I felt her hand grip my shoulder. I spun around quickly and looked at her, my eyes wide with surprise.

The woman had the look of a frightened animal. Her face was pale and drawn, her eyes rimmed with red. I could tell that she had been crying and was about to cry again. Her black hair had not been combed; tangled strands spilled down across her forehead.

I finally recognized her, but it was difficult for me to believe that this was the same Mrs. Chapman who lived in my neighborhood. She now appeared much older than her thirty-odd years, and she was staring into my eyes with an intensity that made me take a couple of steps backward.

"You're Jay Brady, aren't you?" she asked, with desperation edging her voice.

"Yes," I answered, "yes, I am."

"You know my son Robby, don't you?" she said, moving forward and narrowing the space between us.

"Why, yes, I know Robby," I replied. "He's in my eighth-grade science class."

"He's gone!" she blurted out wildly. "We can't find him anywhere!"

"Gone?" I asked. "How long has he been gone?"

"For more than a week," she said as she raised her hand and wiped tears from her face.

"Have you told the police?" I asked.

"Of course we've told the police!" she replied angrily. "And they say Robby probably ran away. But he didn't. I know he didn't! Robby would never run away from us!"

"When was the last time you saw him?"

"Last Tuesday, in Eldon Park. We were having a picnic. Robby was flying his new model airplane. His father and I were sitting at a table watching. We were having a wonderful time, and then...I don't know how it happened, but one minute Robby was there, and the next minute he was gone! We looked everywhere for him. We couldn't find him or his airplane."

"Maybe the police...," I started to say.

"Forget about the police!" she snapped. "They aren't doing anything. They don't care that we've lost our son. They don't care if we ever find him. Please, Jay," she pleaded, "you've got to help us!"

"Me?" I asked in astonishment. "But...how could I help?"

"Talk to Robby's classmates at school," she urged. "Ask if they've seen him or know where he is. Ask his teachers if they've heard something — *anything* about him."

Her chin quivered and tears swelled in her eyes. "He's only thirteen years old," she said. "A boy that young shouldn't be out on his own. Something might happen to him. Please," she begged, "please, help me find my boy!"

"Okay," I agreed halfheartedly, "I'll ask around at school." Then I turned and started walking away.

"Promise you'll help," she called after me.

"I promise," I replied, then immediately wished I hadn't. Why did I promise her anything? I wondered. I hardly knew Robby Chapman. We were in class together, but rarely spoke to each other. Robby was friendly enough, I suppose, but somewhat of a loner. As far as I knew he had only one close friend — Troy Westmore.

But a promise is a promise — and I had promised Mrs. Chapman that I would help her. All I had to do was talk to a few people. That couldn't hurt anything.

When I got to school, the first person I spoke with was my best friend Tyler. I told him about my strange conversation with Mrs. Chapman and how upset she was.

"I haven't seen Robby for some time," Tyler said, brushing a shock of blond hair from his eyes. "It's been at least a week, maybe more. In fact," he said thoughtfully, "I can't remember the last time I did see him. He wasn't in any of my classes."

"Well," I said, "if you hear anything, let me know."

"Okay," Tyler replied. "If I see Robby, I'll tell him you're looking for him." Then he grinned and aimed a playful punch at my shoulder before rushing off to his first class of the day. "See you later," he called to me.

I hurried to Science Class 103, sat down, and opened my notebook. Glancing up at the board, I copied down the daily assignment that my teacher had written there.

I listened carefully during roll call, but Mr. Jansen never mentioned Robby's name. Then I looked toward a desk in the front row — the one where Robby had always sat. I tried to remember what he looked like. To my surprise I found that wasn't easy to do. It took some time for an image of him to form in my mind.

Robby had short-cropped hair, I recalled — black like his mother's — and he wore glasses. He was about my height, but probably a little heavier.

Robby was a real smart kid who always sat at the front of the class, always did his homework, and always knew the answers to the teacher's questions. Now his chair was empty. As I stared at it, Mrs. Chapman's words echoed in my head — *One minute Robby was there, and the next minute he was gone!*

Mr. Jansen's voice brought me back to reality. "Jay, we are waiting for your answer," he said.

I looked up and saw my science teacher staring intensely at me from behind his bifocals.

"Uh...what was the question?" I asked meekly, trying to ignore the snickers of my classmates.

Mr. Jansen repeated the question. Since I had read the assignment, I was able to give him an answer he found acceptable. Still, he sighed and said sarcastically, "Try to stay with us for the rest of the hour, will you, Jay?"

So much for eternal gratitude, I thought. Only two weeks before, Mr. Jansen had said to me, "Thank you, Jay. I appreciate your help with the field trip to the research lab." He had even sent a nice thank-you note to my mother. She had gotten permission for our class to visit the lab at the plant where she worked.

Mr. Jansen's voice soon became a distant sound again, and my thoughts returned to Robby. I craned my neck to get a clear view of his friend Troy, who was sitting several rows across from me. I tried to signal to him to meet me at the door when class ended. He either didn't see my gestures, or he ignored them. With Troy, it was difficult to tell, because he wasn't a very sociable human being. Nevertheless, when the bell sounded, I managed to catch up with him at his locker.

"Hey, Troy, hold on a second," I said, offering him a friendly smile.

"Make it quick," he replied curtly. "I don't want to be late to my next class."

"I just wanted to ask you about Robby Chapman," I explained.

Troy stared at me blankly. "Why should I know anything about him?"

"Well, you and Robby are friends, so I thought you might have some idea of what happened to him."

"Wrong on both counts," he replied. "We were never friends. I hardly knew him." Troy's blue eyes stared coldly into mine. Then he turned abruptly and hurried down the hallway.

I couldn't understand why Troy had denied his friendship with Robby. I had seen them hanging out together lots of times. Why would he lie about that? I wondered. Weird, I thought, really weird. I would soon learn that even weirder things were yet to happen.

I've always said that my mother makes the best macaroni and cheese on this planet. When I walked into the house that evening, I sniffed the wonderful aroma of her special recipe.

"I'm home," I called out. "Smells good!"

"It is good," she called back. "How was your day?"

"Okay, I guess. And yours?" I asked as I entered the kitchen.

"Oh, I don't know," she shrugged. "Some reporters were at the lab again today. They've got their hearts set on proving that the emissions from the new Engine are going to kill everybody. That's probably what they'll print in the paper anyway."

"The emissions can't be that lethal," I reasoned. "You haven't dropped dead yet, and neither have I."

"Those reporters don't realize what a breakthrough the Engine is," she sighed. "If all our tests are successful, we will soon begin using the Engine's chemical reactor to provide electricity for entire cities."

She shook her head in admiration. "I've often wondered how the engineers ever invented the Engine. It's far ahead of all our other technology."

I looked closely at my mother for a few moments. She appeared tired, and rightfully so. She had been putting in a lot of extra hours at the plant since my father moved out last year.

Then my attention turned to a stack of our old newspapers. I sat down by the fireplace and started looking through them. Mom glanced over at me and stopped stirring the macaroni and cheese.

"What are you looking for?" she asked.

"Nothing much. A kid from our school is missing. He's Robby Chapman. Do you remember him?"

"Mary Chapman's son?"

"That's him," I replied.

She frowned thoughtfully. "I think I read about that in the paper the other day. But I had no idea the missing boy was Robby."

"Do you remember which paper?" I asked.

"It was last week sometime — Tuesday, maybe. No, it was Wednesday."

My mother was right. The article had appeared on Wednesday — not on the front page, or even the second page, but buried deep in the paper's innards between advertisements and cartoons. It read:

NORTH VANCOUVER BOY MISSING

A thirteen-year-old boy, five feet three inches tall, with black hair and glasses, vanished in the Grouse Mountain area yesterday. He had been flying his model airplane a short distance from where his mother and father sat eating a picnic lunch. His parents are unsure of the exact time of his disappearance. His mother says, "One minute he was there, and the next minute he was gone." Anyone with information should contact the authorities.

I was amazed! Didn't the story of a missing boy deserve to be on the front-page? Shouldn't it include all the details? The article didn't even mention Robby's name or those of his parents. And why wasn't there a picture of him? And if someone knew something, what authorities could they contact? It didn't say. I tore out the article, folded it, and put it in my pocket.

"Dinner's ready," my mother announced.

I sat down at the table and picked up my fork. When I looked up, I saw Mom smiling at me.

"Try not to worry," she said reassuringly. "The police will find Robby."

Will they? I thought to myself. I sighed inwardly, feeling totally helpless. How could I keep from worrying about Robby? The look on Mrs. Chapman's stricken face invaded my mind. Her voice bored its way into my thoughts — "Please help me find my boy!" she had pleaded.

The macaroni was delicious, but I couldn't finish it. I had lost my appetite.

On Saturday morning I rode my bicycle to Eldon Park. I had no idea of what I expected to find there. Maybe I was hoping to discover some clues the police had missed, but I knew that was highly unlikely. Maybe I just wanted to try to arrange a more complete picture in my mind of what might have happened the day Robby disappeared.

After I got off my bicycle, I stood still for some time, surveying the scene before me. It was a cool October morning. Although the air was edged with the chill of autumn, the sun shone brightly on me from an open sky. I strolled across the grass, looking directly at the playground ahead of me.

To my left was an empty swing set. Its hinges squeaked as the swings swayed in ghostly motion in the breeze. A battered old merry-go-round, paint cracked and peeling, stood beyond that. On the right was a metal sliding board, its dented surface gleaming from beneath a layer of pine needles.

An eerie feeling crept over me as I looked at the empty playground. For a few moments, I could almost hear the sounds of children playing. The air echoed with their shrieks of excitement as they spun in wild circles on the merry-go-round and careened down the slide. Then the sounds were gone.

Above me, several ravens were perched in the trees. They sat still, as if suspended in time and space, not turning their heads to the left or the right. All the same I could feel their dark eyes watching me.

What really happened here last Tuesday? I wondered. I tried to visualize the scene in my mind's eye. It had been a warm day, so Robby Chapman had brought his newest remote-control model airplane to the park to try it out. Mrs. Chapman had packed a picnic lunch.

My gaze fell on the picnic tables to my right. The Chapmans had sat at one of them, eating sandwiches while their son ran across the grassy field. Robby was probably looking up, watching his aircraft move in lazy dips and wide circles high above. Perhaps his attention was so fixed on his plane that he had wandered too far away from his parents — maybe toward the edge of the field...

One minute he was there, and the next minute he was gone.

There was a wooded area a short distance away. I walked across the field toward the trees. The wind felt colder now, and I buttoned my jacket. When I reached the woods, I stared upward. Sunlight filtered through the branches of the pine and hemlock trees that stood before me. I took several steps beyond the line of trees, and then I saw it — a narrow dirt path that led into the woods. I had never before noticed the path.

My pulse quickened. Had Robby wandered onto that path? Had he disappeared in these woods? If he had, perhaps there was something in there — something everyone else had missed. Then I grinned at my own foolishness. If the path had been so easy for me to find, surely the police had already seen it and searched its length. Still, I decided to take a look for myself.

I stepped onto the path and moved quietly into the woods. The smell of pine needles filled my nostrils as I walked between the old and weathered trunks of the evergreens. About fifty yards into the woods, I reached a small clearing that was situated on a high bluff.

It was a glorious view! I stood on the bluff and looked at the breathtaking scene of the forested hills beyond. Autumn leaves, set ablaze by the sun's reflection, glowed orange in the morning light.

The bluff fell straight down to a deep valley below. As I moved closer to the edge of the precipice, I was reminded that it would be a far fall to the floor of the valley. I wondered if Robby had stepped too close to the edge and fallen.

On the ground beneath my feet, dry leaves rustled, stirred by the breeze. Suddenly an uneasy feeling crept over me. Perhaps it was the solitude of the place that made me apprehensive, but somehow I knew I was being watched.

I turned around and saw a park bench in the center of the clearing. An old man with white hair was seated there. He wore a gray jacket and clasped a cane tightly in his weathered hands. My first reaction was to hurry back to the park and leave quickly. But I didn't.

"Good morning," I forced myself to say.

The man nodded his head. "Morning," he replied and gave me a warm, friendly smile.

I smiled back at him, but I was still nervous. Suddenly I felt uncomfortably close to the edge of the bluff, so I took a few steps away from it.

"Do you come here often?" I asked, trying to sound at ease.

"Whenever I can," he answered. His voice was deep and soothing, almost musical.

"It's a beautiful view," I commented.

"Hmmm," he agreed. "There is no place like it in the universe."

"I suppose you're right," I said.

"I know I am right," he insisted. "And no matter how many times I see it, it is never the same. It is always changing."

"It looks like untouched territory," I said somewhat awkwardly, "except, of course, for that smokestack at the plant in the valley."

I pointed to the tall chimney. It rose like a gleaming steel finger and was releasing a jagged stream of smoke into the air.

"My mother works there," I said. "It's mainly a science research lab. That smoke comes from the new Engine's chemical reactor. Mom says the Engine is far advanced to anything we now have. It provides an amazing amount of energy and gives off almost no pollution."

"Hmmm," the old man replied.

I suspected I was boring him with talk about the Engine. Anyway, it was time I asked the questions I had in mind and then got out of there.

"If you come here often," I began, "perhaps you've seen one of my friends. He sometimes flies his model airplanes in the park. He's my age and about my height, except he has black hair and wears glasses." My voice faded to nothingness as the old man turned and fixed his gaze directly on me. I shivered, realizing I could not look away.

"Robby Chapman is all right," he said quietly. "Do not worry about him."

My throat went dry, and a cold feeling went through me. I stood there rooted to the spot.

Then something sped past my face. I jumped back as a small red object almost hit me. It dropped to the ground just beyond me and rolled to a stop. It was a child's ball. Instinctively, I reached down and picked it up. A young boy ran into the clearing and held out his hands. I tossed the ball to him.

"Thanks," he called to me as he darted back down the path toward the playground.

When I found the courage to look back, the bench was empty; the old man was gone. I heard the flutter of wings above my head and looked up. A raven was circling in the air above me. Silhouetted in streams of sunlight, it spread it wings and soared beyond the treetops. Then it was gone.

The old man had said, *Robby Chapman is all right. Do not worry about him.* But, how did he know that? Why would he say such a thing? Had the police already seen the old man? Had they talked to him and questioned him?

My breath formed tiny puffs of steam in front of me as I left the park and bicycled toward home. I was frightened, to say the least. Reaching my driveway, I turned, half expecting to see the old man had materialized somewhere behind me. He was nowhere in sight. Leaving my bicycle on the ground, I stepped inside the house, then hurried to the kitchen, where I picked up the phone and dialed a number. After the sound of three rings, a woman's voice answered, "Police Department."

I told her I had information about Robby Chapman. She put me on hold. A few moments later, another voice came on the line.

"Hello, this is Constable Clint McAllister. How may I help you?"

I told him about being at Eldon Park that morning — the place where Robby Chapman had disappeared. And I told him I had met a strange old man. "He not only knows Robby's name," I explained, "but he also said that Robby was all right. I think he knows where Robby is."

"Why were you asking about Robby Chapman?" the constable inquired curtly.

"I know him from school. He's in my science class, and..."

"How old are you?" the constable interrupted me.

"Thirteen," I answered.

"Listen, kid," he warned, "if there's one thing we don't need on this case, it's a thirteen-year-old boy who is trying to play detective. Don't you know that snooping around and questioning strange old men in parks can be dangerous? Now,

you tell me what this guy looks like, then you mind your own business and leave the investigation to the police. Do you understand me?''

"Yessir," I replied. Then I carefully described the old man to him — white hair, gray jacket, and carrying a cane, "and he knows Robby's name," I repeated emphatically.

"That doesn't mean a thing," he said. "He probably remembers it from the article in the newspaper. But we'll try to find this old man and ask him a few questions." Then he wanted to know my name and phone number. As soon as I had given the information to him, I heard the phone click in my ear, signaling an abrupt end to our conversation.

I was annoyed by the way the constable had talked to me. And something else bothered me, too. I suddenly realized the old man couldn't have learned Robby's name from the newspaper. Robby's name was *never* mentioned in the article!

I raised the telephone receiver to call Constable McAllister again, then decided I had better not. I replaced the receiver on the phone and walked over to the refrigerator. A note from my mother was taped on its door. "Jay," it read, "I have to work late at the plant tonight. Dinner is in the frige. Love, Mom."

On Monday I became even more disturbed. When Mr. Jansen called the roll, he didn't say Stacy Kirby's name. I looked over at Stacy's desk and tried to remember when I had last seen her in class. I couldn't recall. When I looked around the room, I noticed four more empty desks. Were those extra desks? I wondered. Or were other students missing, too? As soon as class ended, I approached Mr. Jansen.

"What can I do for you, Jay?" he asked.

"I was wondering, Sir, is Stacy Kirby sick?"

"How should I know?" he replied matter-of-factly.

"Well, she wasn't here today."

"Apparently not," he said.

"I don't think she's been here for several days."

Mr. Jansen frowned at me. "We'll see," he said, opening his record book. Together, we scanned the page until we found Stacy's name. A black line had been drawn through it.

"Oh, I just remembered," he said. "She moved away last week. Stacy Kirby is all right. Do not worry about her."

I looked at the class list again and saw that Robby Chapman's name was crossed out, too. And three other students had lines drawn through their names. They were Lynn Francis, Wesley Evans, and William Parker.

Mr. Jansen closed the book and placed it inside his briefcase. "Now, Jay, please don't forget your homework assignment," he instructed as he pushed past me and rushed out the door.

While they were still fresh in my mind, I hurriedly wrote down the three students' names on a piece of paper. Then I stared at them for a few moments. Strangely enough, I couldn't remember what any of these students looked like.

On my way home that afternoon, I turned the corner of Cliff Ridge Drive and walked down the curving dead-end street where Stacy Kirby had lived. I couldn't understand why she left without saying good-bye to me. We were pretty good friends.

Stacy's house was at the end of the street. A large maple tree stood at the edge of the yard, its leaves turning orange and red. Beneath it, a stocky, middle-aged man was raking the leaves that had fallen from its boughs.

"Hi, there," I said, giving him a friendly smile. "I was wondering if you knew where the Kirby family has moved?"

Leaning on his rake, he gave me an amused look and replied, "As far as I know, they haven't moved anywhere." Seeing the look of confusion on my face, he stuck out his hand and introduced himself. "I'm John Kirby."

I shook his hand. "I'm Jay Brady. Are you Stacy's father?" I asked.

"Well...yes...I am," he answered hesitantly.

"Stacy wasn't at school today," I told him. "I wondered if she might be sick."

Mr. Kirby paused and stared thoughtfully into the distance. He seemed to be having trouble concentrating, but finally replied, "I don't think she's ill."

There was an uncomfortable pause. "May I see her?" I asked.

"No," he answered, "she's not at home right now."

"Where is she?" I persisted.

"Well, I'm not sure," he said. "I'll ask my wife." He turned toward the house and called out, "Lorna, there's a boy here who wants to see Stacy. Where did she go?"

15

Mrs. Kirby came to the window and called back, "I don't know where Stacy is. I thought you knew."

"How would I know?" he replied. "I haven't seen her in maybe two weeks, or was it sometime last year? I just can't remember."

"Isn't that the strangest thing," Mrs. Kirby said quietly as she leaned out the window and looked up and down the street. "You know, I thought about Stacy just yesterday, and I said to myself, 'I should find out where she is.' And then it just slipped my mind. But I think she'll come back before long."

Mr. Kirby turned to me and said, "When Stacy gets home, I'll tell her you stopped by." Then he looked at me with a blank stare and commented, "Stacy is all right. Do not worry about her."

He started raking leaves again, leaving me to stand there open-mouthed, realizing I had heard a similar comment from the old man and one from Mr. Jansen, too: *Robby is all right. Stacy is all right. Do not worry...* At this point, how could I *not* worry about them?

As I walked home, I did some mental backtracking, trying to recall the last time I had seen Stacy and Robby. I remembered Stacy had sat beside me on the bus during our field trip to the plant. Had Robby gone on the trip, too? I didn't know. And how about the other missing students? I couldn't recall if I had seen them there either.

Then the thought suddenly struck me: there was a way to find out who had toured the plant that day. All of us had been required to sign a guest book. I hurried into the house and phoned my mother. She answered almost immediately and said, "Hello."

"Hi, Mom, it's Jay. Will you do me a favor?"

"Sure," she replied. "What is it?"

"Could you take a look at the guest registry at the plant. I need the names of the kids who were on the field trip with me. It's very important."

"Okay, I'll go to the reception room and get it, then call you back in a few minutes."

I waited impatiently. As soon as the phone rang, I grabbed it. While Mom slowly read off the names, I scribbled down each one on a piece of paper.

"And Mr. Jansen's signature is the last one on the page," she told me.

"Thanks, Mom," I said and hung up. Then I carefully studied the list. Both Stacy and Robby were on it, and so were Lynn Francis, Wesley Evans, and William Parker. All five of them had been on the field trip!

To paraphrase Mrs. Chapman: *One day they were here, and the next day they were gone.* But, gone where? I wondered. I folded the list of names and put it in my pocket.

On Tuesday morning, I stepped into my science classroom the minute the bell rang. I knew immediately that something was wrong because the number of students in class had grown even smaller. Again, as I looked at each empty desk, I had trouble visualizing the students who had sat there.

Mr. Jansen stood behind his neatly organized desk, pen in hand, and took attendance. He called out only the names of those students who were present. The empty desks stood as mute reminders that ten students were now missing.

I looked about the room to see if my classmates had noticed the high absentee rate. No one seemed disturbed. And Mr. Jansen began the day's lesson as if nothing at all had changed.

About halfway through the hour, he left the room to talk to another teacher. I hurried to his desk and opened his record book. Another five names had been crossed out. I scribbled them on a scrap of paper and returned to my desk. None of my classmates seemed to notice what I had just done.

I pulled the guest list from my pocket and found that the five additional students had also visited the plant. As I checked off their names, they seemed vaguely familiar. When I spoke the names aloud, there was a tugging at my mind as if I had heard them a long time ago. But for the life of me, I couldn't remember what the students looked like.

I was late to my second-hour history class on purpose. What was currently happening to the missing students was far more important than today's lesson on the Middle Ages. So I stopped by the school office instead, where a secretary saw me and wandered over to where I stood.

"May I help you?" she asked in a bored voice.

I placed the list of missing students on the counter top for her to see. "I'd like to find out where these students are," I told her.

She glanced at the list with disinterest, then said, "We are not allowed to give out such information to students."

I decided to reinforce my position. "All *ten* of these students are missing!" I declared bluntly.

That caught her attention. "Wait here," she said, then turned and hurried into the principal's office. Through the open door, I could see she was having a serious discussion with Mr. Patterson. Between their whispers, they would turn and look in my direction. I tried to appear relaxed.

While I waited, an office clerk sat down before the computer and turned it on. For a few moments she hesitated. I realized she must have forgotten the access password, for she opened a drawer in the computer stand and looked inside. Then she shut the drawer, keyed in a password, and watched as data flowed across the screen.

Finally, the secretary came out of the principal's office. "Mr. Patterson will see you now," she informed me.

I followed her to his office and stepped inside. She closed the door behind me. Mr. Patterson's spacious office was dominated by a large wooden desk at one end. He motioned for me to sit down across from him.

"You're Jay Brady, right?" he said with a friendly smile. "What seems to be the problem?"

I cleared my throat, then said hesitantly, "Uh... some students are missing from my science class."

"Absent," he corrected me cheerfully. "They probably have the flu, or something."

"But there are *ten* of them," I said. "I don't think all ten are sick."

"Do you know for certain that they are not?" he asked.

"I know Robby Chapman is not home with the flu," I blurted out.

Mr. Patterson's gaze darkened. "Has Mrs. Chapman been talking to you, too?" he wanted to know.

I hesitated too long before answering.

"I should have known!" he complained, raising his hands in despair. "That woman is going to drive all of us crazy! She phones here every day!"

"She's concerned about her son," I said sharply.

"Well, of course, she is," he agreed, his voice becoming more understanding. "All of us are concerned. But this is a police matter. So we should let the police take care of the Robby Chapman case."

"All right," I replied, "but what about Stacy Kirby?"

"What about Stacy?" he frowned.

"She's missing, too," I said.

"I believe Stacy went to live with relatives in Seattle," he informed me.

"If she did, her father and mother don't know about it," I replied quickly.

"No, they wouldn't," Mr. Patterson explained, shaking his head sadly. "You see, Stacy's parents are very confused people; they have beginning Alzheimer's disease."

"I had no idea," I said, recalling the strange comments the Kirbys had made the day before.

"You see what I mean, Jay," Mr. Patterson told me, his voice returning to very friendly tones. "There are so many unusual situations, so many complications we have to deal with at school. Sometimes students move. Sometimes they have family problems. We hear about all of them. I can assure you, being the principal of a school is not an easy job."

"I'm sure it's not," I said, "but . . . "

"But what?" he asked curtly, becoming a bit annoyed.

"What about the other students?"

"The other students are none of your concern, Jay. They are all right. Do not worry about them."

The statements about the missing students replayed in my brain. Again, I realized all were too similar to be coincidences.

Robby Chapman is all right. Do not worry about him.

Stacy Kirby is all right. Do not worry about her.

They are all right. Do not worry about them.

At that point it became apparent to me that Mr. Patterson did not wish to discuss matters further. "Thanks for your time," I said. "I have to get to class now." As I was leaving, I glanced over my shoulder and saw the secretary hurry into the principal's office. They were watching me, and I knew they were talking about me, too.

In keeping with our noontime ritual, I joined Tyler for lunch in the cafeteria and sat down beside him.

"Hey, Tyler," I whispered.

Seeing the concerned look on my face, he whispered back, "What's up, Jay?"

"Listen, Tyler, I need your help. Could you stay after school with me tonight?"

"Why?"

"I want to check on some names that are listed in the computer that's located in the front office."

"Are you serious?" he asked in amazement.

"Yes," I told him, "very serious. We'll have to stay until everyone else leaves the building. Are you with me?"

Tyler gave me a questioning look. "Does this have anything to do with the Robby Chapman thing?" he wondered.

"It's not only about Robby. There are now *ten* students missing," I told him.

"Listen, Jay," Tyler said, starting to sound a bit nervous. "Maybe you should give it a rest. I mean, this thing about Robby is all you've been talking about for the last few days."

"Are you with me or not?" I demanded impatiently.

"Well...sure...I'm with you," he answered slowly.

I could tell by the tone of his voice that he was not too enthusiastic about the idea. But I needed his help, so I quickly said, "Okay, then meet me here in the cafeteria right after school."

Tyler nodded his head in agreement.

Tyler met me as he had promised. But I could tell something was wrong.

"What's the matter?" I asked.

"Jay, I'm sorry, but I can't stay," he replied. "My grandma's in Lion's Gate Hospital. She's real sick. My parents are in front of school right now to pick me up."

"No problem," I lied, waving him aside. "I hope your grandma gets better soon."

"If you'll wait until tomorrow evening, I'll stay with you then," he offered.

"Okay," I replied, pretending to agree.

As I watched Tyler hurry away, I felt as if he had deserted me. But I didn't intend to wait one more day. What had to be done, would be done tonight, and I would do it alone.

I took a deep breath, steeling myself with determination as I walked toward the front office. I tried to appear casual as I strolled past the door. Then, when I was sure no one was watching, I slipped inside a supply closet that was across the hall from the office. I left the door slightly ajar so I could keep an eye on things. I stayed there, out of sight, and waited.

By four o'clock the halls were almost empty. I heard the last few students close their lockers and listened to their departing footsteps echo down the hallways. Then reverberating crashes announced their departure as outside doors were slammed shut.

The last secretary finally left, and I saw the janitor push his cleaning trolley into the office. When he had finished his work, he exited the room, rolling his trolley ahead of him. And what luck! He had left the office door open!

When I heard his vacuum cleaner roar to life in a distant classroom, I seized the opportunity to slip quietly across the hall and into the office. Then I tucked myself under one of the desks.

Time passed slowly. More than once I considered giving up the whole idea and going home. But I forced myself to remain where I was. I had come this far. I couldn't stop now.

Finally, all the cleaning sounds ended, and I heard the classroom doors being shut one by one. I held my breath, listening to the janitor's approaching footsteps. I prayed he would not come into the room where I was hiding.

Only after I heard him close the office door and turn the key in the lock did I relax a bit. And when the last outside door banged shut, I released a long sigh of relief, knowing the janitor was gone for the night.

Now an overpowering invasion of aloneness surrounded me. All was quiet, except for the sounds of my breathing and the popping and cracking of the old building's settling floors.

I stood up and stretched my cramped legs. Then I hurried to the computer terminal and sat down, thumbed on the START button, and waited while the screen flickered to life. But when I tried to access the student files, the program instructed me to enter a password. Remembering where the office clerk had found the word, I opened the drawer and looked inside. Only one piece of paper was there, and on it was typed one word in large letters. It said —

ROLLCALL

I keyed in *ROLLCALL,* and the computer welcomed me as "Mrs. Collins." That amused me, and I smiled with satisfaction at my success. But when I tried to access the student files for Mr. Jansen's Science Class 103, my smile faded. *Another* password was requested.

I looked in the drawer again. Typed on the back of the paper was a number and a word —

103 RAVEN

So I keyed in that code.

Bingo! It worked! My eyes widened with delight as information scrolled across the screen. Soon I was able to access Robby Chapman's file. I scanned through all of his data, pausing only long enough to scribble down his locker number and combination on a notepad. Then, at the bottom of Robby's file, I saw a single word. It said —

CHANGED

What was that supposed to mean? I wondered. Frowning, I accessed Stacy Kirby's file and saw the same word —

CHANGED

I quickly checked the files of the other missing students. A feeling of uneasiness came over me after I discovered that all contained the word —

CHANGED

Normal curiosity, of course, led me to my own file. I had to know what it said. As I accessed the file, my fingers trembled nervously on the keyboard. I hurriedly scrolled to the bottom of the screen. Three words met my gaze —

TO BE CHANGED

My uneasiness turned to fear of the unknown. I flipped the OFF button, stood up, and backed away from the computer. Every bit of common sense I possessed told me to get out of the school building right away. But I stayed, knowing there was one more thing I had to do. Taking the note from the pad, I went to the office door, unlocked it, and stepped into the hallway. The door snapped shut behind me.

The building was dark and quiet. As I made my way down the hall, the corridor stretched out before me like a long tunnel. Distorted shadows moved at the edges of my vision, but when I looked, nothing was there. I was frightened for sure, and my mind was whirling with questions.

TO BE CHANGED

What did that mean? Changed how?

I turned the corner into a connecting hall and found Robby's locker almost immediately. I looked at the combination on the note; my fingers fumbled as I tried to enter the numbers correctly. Finally I succeeded, and the lock yielded. Metal grated against metal as I lifted the handle and pulled at the locker door. It stuck momentarily, then creaked loudly on its hinges when I yanked it open.

Books and loose papers were crammed inside. Discarded gym clothes were stuffed under the heap. And then, I looked up and saw it. On the top shelf rested a small, battery-powered model airplane. I reached up and took it from the locker. The plane looked new. I wondered if it was the one Robby had flown the day he disappeared. My thoughts were abruptly interrupted when footsteps sounded in the front hallway.

Being as quiet as possible, I pushed the locker door closed. Then I darted around a corner and stood out of sight. As the footsteps came closer, I held my breath and clutched Robby's airplane tightly in my hands.

"Why is it taking so long?" I heard someone ask. It was Mr. Patterson's voice.

"It's a slow process," a second voice answered. "You must be patient." The voice was deep and soothing; I had heard it before. In seconds I realized it was the voice of the old man I had talked to in Eldon Park!

"We will take care of the changes," the old man continued. "Your job is to make sure everything looks normal at school. We do not want people to worry."

"Some are already worried," Mr. Patterson insisted, "like Jay Brady for instance."

"Jay Brady will be all right. Do not worry about him," replied the old man.

Now I was *really* frightened! Mr. Patterson and the old man were discussing me personally! I shook with fear, but didn't make a sound as the two men continued down the front hall, away from me. Soon their voices faded into the distance.

After a while I decided it was safe to leave, and I stepped quietly from my hiding place. But as I crept down the darkened hall, I bumped into a trash can. Its metal lid fell to the floor with a crash.

"Hey! Who's there?" I heard Mr. Patterson bellow loudly.

I didn't answer; I just ran! I could hear the two men coming after me; the sound of their footsteps mingled with my own, and the tapping of the old man's cane added to my fright.

I was clearly the faster runner, but in my panic, I turned a corner too sharply, slipped on a freshly waxed floor, and slammed my right shoulder into a wall. I saw double doors just ahead of me and raced toward them. Then I remembered — they would be locked. I had to find another way out!

As I rushed into the cafeteria, an escape route came to my mind. The windows in the room were locked from the inside by simple latches. I could easily open them. Sprinting past a table and leaping over stools, I grabbed hold of the latch on the nearest window and wrenched it upward. The lower section of the panel of glass swung open. Still holding the model airplane in my hand, I scrambled through the opening, jumped to the ground, and sped across the open school yard.

Now I was terrified! Somehow Mr. Patterson and the old man knew each other, and both were involved with the disappearances of the students. But why? I wondered. What were they up to?

By the time I reached our house, I was out of breath. As soon as I was inside, I relocked the door securely behind me. I peeked between the curtains and looked through the front window. I saw no one outside. "Good! I wasn't followed!" I told myself. Then I took a couple of deep breaths and tried to clear my thoughts. I knew I had to do something, but what?

"Call the police!" I finally reasoned. Maybe Constable McAllister would know what to do." I ran to the kitchen, grabbed the phone, and dialed the number.

"Police Department," a woman's voice answered.

"Constable McAllister, please," I said.

"I'm sorry, but Constable McAllister isn't here tonight."

"Where can I reach him?" I asked.

"You can't," she replied. "He was in a car accident earlier today, and he's in the hospital."

"Well," I said, sighing with frustration, "I need to talk to *someone*. I have information regarding the Robby Chapman case."

"The what case?" she asked.

"The Robby Chapman case," I repeated. "Robby was the boy who disappeared in Eldon Park two weeks ago."

"Please hold for a minute," the woman instructed. After a brief pause, she returned to the phone and said, "I'm sorry, but we have no record of a missing person named Robby Chapman. What is your name?" she wanted to know.

I didn't answer; I just slammed down the receiver in exasperation. Mrs. Chapman had been right: the police had already forgotten about Robby! And what about the constable? Had he really been in an accident, or was he missing, too?

When I walked to the refrigerator, I saw another note from my mother was taped to the door. It read: "Jay, I have to work late again. Dinner is in the frige. Love, Mom." I didn't even open the refrigerator door. I had no desire to eat anything. I just felt tired, terribly tired.

Mom's note began to trouble me, too, when I suddenly realized that I had not seen her for three days. She had returned home each night after I was asleep and left the house each morning before I awakened. Or that's what I had supposed. Now I wondered if she had been home at all.

I worried all evening, wondering if Mom was all right. About 9:00 I dialed her office. The receptionist told me Mom was in a meeting. So I left a message for her to call home as soon as possible. But my mother didn't call that night, and she didn't come home either.

Before I left for school the next morning, I phoned the plant again. I was told that Mom was in another meeting. I left a message for her to return my call that evening.

On the way to school, I stopped by Robby's house. His mother was standing in the driveway. I was glad to see that she was looking much better than the last time I had seen her. She even smiled at me.

"How are you?" she asked cheerfully.

"Fine," I replied. "I wanted you to know that I asked around at school about Robby. No one seems to know where he is. But I found this model airplane in his locker. Do you think it's the one he had at Eldon Park?"

"I wouldn't know," she answered as she reached out and took the airplane. "Robby has so many models.

"So you've been looking for Robby," she continued. "That's very nice of you, Jay, but don't put

yourself to so much trouble.'' Then she gave me a blank stare and said, "Robby is all right. Do not worry about him."

I stared back at her in amazement. "How do you know for sure that he's all right?" I gasped. "He's missing, remember? And the police can't find him! And I met an old man in Eldon Park who said he knew Robby, and..."

"Now, Jay," she interrupted, "you've gotten yourself all upset over nothing. Say, it's getting late," she said, looking at her wrist watch. "You had better be on your way to school. You'll miss your first class if you don't leave now."

I was numb with confusion. When I arrived for science class, I was even more stunned to find that I was the only student in the room. I walked to the front row, but didn't sit down.

Mr. Jansen was at the board, writing out the day's assignment. Other than the chalk squeaking against the surface, there were no sounds — no early morning chatter from students, no friendly laughter, no sounds of papers being shuffled or books being opened and closed.

I watched Mr. Jansen turn from the board and pick up his class record book. He cleared his throat, the way he always did before taking roll call.

"Jay Brady," he called out.

I didn't answer. When he looked up and saw me, he frowned. "Speak up, Jay," he said crossly as he put a check by my name, "or next time I'll mark you absent."

I waited for him to call the other students' names. Instead, he closed the record book and placed it on his desk. Without looking inside that book, I already knew what it meant: the names of all my classmates had been crossed out — everyone's name but mine.

I suddenly heard the sound of fluttering wings, and the door opened. I turned to see the old man walk into the room. He stopped before me and smiled his friendly smile.

Two other men entered and walked straight to Mr. Jansen. My science teacher didn't move or even blink his eyes. It appeared as if he had been frozen to the spot. He looked like a wax dummy, standing totally motionless at the front of the classroom.

Without a word, the two men picked up Mr. Jansen. As if he were no more than a department store mannequin, they carried him from the room.

Now I was alone with the old man. I was tempted to make a mad dash for the door. But then he smiled at me again, and my fears disappeared immediately. I just felt relaxed.

"Why have you taken all the students away?" I asked quietly.

"We have taken them away for their own good," he replied kindly. "They are sick. We are in the process of curing their sickness."

"What's wrong with them?" I wanted to know.

"There was an unfortunate accident while your science class was touring the plant," he explained. "A hairline crack developed in the Engine, and it released a lethal toxin into the air. Everyone in the building was affected — employees and visitors alike, even Mr. Jansen. We are removing the toxins from their bodies."

"Then, you've kidnaped my classmates!" I said.

"We only borrowed them," he explained calmly. "The detoxification process takes time. Robby was first because he was poisoned the most. His disappearance caused more commotion than we would have liked. But we have everything under complete control again."

"You make people forget things, too, don't you?" I said.

"We do not want them to worry," he replied with a gentle smile.

"But, how do you make them forget?"

"By using ultrasonic sounds, we erase portions of their memories."

"Where did you come from?" I asked.

"From a planet in a distant galaxy that is several thousand light years from Earth."

"And why have you come here?" I wanted to know.

"To help you human beings," he replied. "Our knowledge is far greater than yours. The Engine is our creation. It generates the power necessary for our advanced technology. Earth is just one of many planets where we have built our Engines."

It took some time for the old man's words to sink into my mind.

"What about my mother?" I finally asked.

"She was poisoned, too," he said, "but we are already taking care of her. Your mother is all right. Do not worry about her."

"Will I be all right, too?"

"Of course you will," he assured me. "Once you have been detoxified, you will be as good as new. It is a painless process. In fact, it is a rather pleasant one. And when it is completed, you will forget that all of this ever happened. Now, Jay," he said, "you must come with me at once."

The old man smiled his warm, friendly smile, convincing me that I could trust him totally. And when he turned toward the door, I put on my jacket and willingly followed him. As we proceeded down the hallway, the end of the long corridor opened up before us, and we stepped into the expanse of space beyond.

There was a strong wind blowing through the trees in Eldon Park, carrying with it the warning of approaching winter. The chill of frost in the air made me shiver. When I heard the rustle of leaves below me, something from the past tugged at my memory. But I couldn't recall what it was.

"It will be easier for you when you have forgotten everything," the old man had told me.

Maybe he was right, but sometimes I felt uneasy about that — I mean, forgetting *everything*. The others didn't seem to mind, not even my mother. But we never discussed it anymore. Besides, I no longer could distinguish Mom from the others. And I don't think she recognized me either. Oh, well...I tried not to think about that.

The view from above the treetops was far more breathtaking than any I had seen from the ground. As I gazed over the sweeping landscape, a slim silver structure caught my eye — a smokestack made

of steel. From its chimney top, a jagged stream of smoke curled slowly upward. For a moment I was reminded of a day when I had stood on the cliff and looked out over the valley...but...

Suddenly, down, down, down I plummeted!

"Do not think of the past," the old man had warned. "It will interfere with your flying."

As quickly as I could, I erased all thoughts from my mind and concentrated only on my flying. I stretched out my wings and caught the wind beneath my shiny black feathers. Then I soared upward to join the other ravens in the autumn sky.

"It *is* a beautiful view, isn't it?" a woman said as she looked up and saw us flying above the trees.

"Hmmm," the old man agreed. "There is no place like it in the universe. And it is never the same — it is always changing."

BOOKS FOR STUDENTS

– WINNERS OF THE NATIONAL WRITTEN &

by Aruna Chandrasekhar, age 9
Houston, Texas

A touching and timely story! When the lives of many otters are threatened by a huge oil spill, a group of concerned people come to their rescue. Wonderful illustrations.
Printed Full Color
ISBN 0-933849-33-8

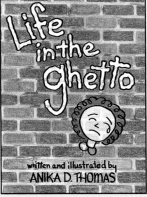

by Anika D. Thomas, age 13
Pittsburgh, Pennsylvania

A compelling autobiography! A young girl's heartrending account of growing up in a tough, inner-city neighborhood. The illustrations match the mood of this gripping story.
Printed Two Colors
ISBN 0-933849-34-6

by Cara Reichel, age 15
Rome, Georgia

Elegant and eloquent! A young stonecutter vows to create a great statue for his impoverished village. But his fame almost stops him from fulfilling that promise.
Printed Two Colors
ISBN 0-933849-35-4

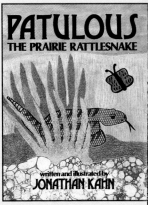

by Jonathan Kahn, age 9
Richmond Heights, Ohio

A fascinating nature story! While Patulous, a prairie rattlesnake, searches for food, he must try to avoid the claws and fangs of his own enemies.
Printed Full Color
ISBN 0-933849-36-2

by Adam Moore, age 9
Broken Arrow, Oklahoma

A remarkable true story! When Adam was eight years old, he fell and ran an arrow into his head. With rare insight and humor, he tells of his ordeal and his amazing recovery.
Printed Two Colors
ISBN 0-933849-24-9

by Michael Aushenker, age 19
Ithaca, New York

Chomp! Chomp! When Arthur forgets to feed his goat, the animal eats everything in sight. A very funny story — good to the last bite. The illustrations are terrific.
Printed Full Color
ISBN 0-933849-28-1

by Leslie Ann MacKeen, age 9
Winston-Salem, North Carolina

Loaded with fun and puns! When Jeremiah T. Fitz's car stops running, several animals offer suggestions for fixing it. The results are hilarious. The illustrations are charming.
Printed Full Color
ISBN 0-933849-19-2

by Elizabeth Haidle, age 13
Beaverton, Oregon

A very touching story! The grumpiest Elfkin learns to cherish the friendship of others after he helps an injured snail and befriends an orphaned boy. Absolutely beautiful
Printed Full Color
ISBN 0-933849-20-6

by Amy Hagstrom, age 9
Portola, California

An exciting western! When a boy and an old Indian try to save a herd of wild ponies, they discover a lost canyon and see the mystical vision of the Great White Stallion.
Printed Full Color
ISBN 0-933849-15-X

by Isaac Whitlatch, age 11
Casper, Wyoming

The true confessions of a devout vegetable hater! Isaac tells ways to avoid and dispose of the "slimy green things." His colorful illustrations provide a salad of laughter and mirth.
Printed Full Color
ISBN 0-933849-16-8

by Dav Pilkey, age 19
Cleveland, Ohio

A thought-provoking parable! Two kings halt an arms race and learn to live in peace. This outstanding book launched Dav's career. He now has seven more books published.
Printed Full Color
ISBN 0-933849-22-2

by Karen Kerber, age 12
St. Louis, Missouri

A delightfully playful book! The text is loaded with clever alliterations and gentle humor. Karen's brightly colored illustrations are composed of wiggly and waggly strokes of genius
Printed Full Color
ISBN 0-933849-29-X

Your Students Will Love These Wonderful Books

BY STUDENTS!®

ILLUSTRATED BY... AWARDS FOR STUDENTS –

by Jayna Miller, age 19
Zanesville, Ohio

The funniest Halloween ever! When Hammer the Rabbit takes all the treats, his friends get even. Their hilarious scheme includes a haunted house and mounds of chocolate.
Printed Full Color
ISBN 0-933849-37-0

by Lauren Peters, age 7
Kansas City, Missouri

The Christmas that almost wasn't! When Santa Claus takes a vacation, Mrs. Claus and the elves go on strike. Toys aren't made. Cookies aren't baked. Super illustrations.
Printed Full Color
ISBN 0-933849-25-7

by Michael Cain, age 11
Annapolis, Maryland

A glorious tale of adventure! To become a knight, a young man must face a beast in the forest, a spell-binding witch, and a giant bird that guards a magic oval crystal.
Printed Full Color
ISBN 0-933849-26-5

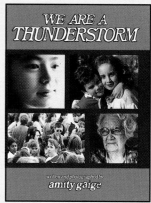

by Amity Gaige, age 16
Reading, Pennsylvania

A lyrical blend of poetry and photographs! Amity's sensitive poems offer thought-provoking ideas and amusing insights. This lovely book is one to be savored and enjoyed.
Printed Full Color
ISBN 0-933849-27-3

Heidi Salter, age 19
Berkeley, California

Spooky and wonderful! To save her vivid imagination, a young girl must confront the Great Grey Grimly himself. The narrative is filled with suspense. Vibrant illustrations.
Printed Full Color
ISBN 0-933849-21-4

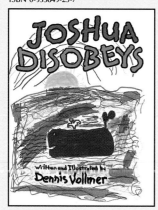

by Dennis Vollmer, age 6
Grove, Oklahoma

A baby whale's curiosity gets him into a lot of trouble. GUINNESS BOOK OF RECORDS lists Dennis as the youngest author/illustrator of a published book.
Printed Full Color
ISBN 0-933849-12-5

by Lisa Gross, age 12
Santa Fe, New Mexico

A touching story of self-esteem! A puppy is laughed at because of his unusual appearance. His search for acceptance is told with sensitivity and humor. Wonderful illustrations.
Printed Full Color
ISBN 0-933849-13-3

by Stacy Chbosky, age 14
Pittsburgh, Pennsylvania

A powerful plea for freedom! This emotion-packed story of a young slave touches an essential part of the human spirit. Made into a film by Disney Educational Productions.
Printed Full Color
ISBN 0-933849-14-1

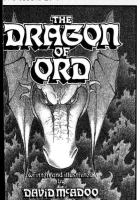

David McAdoo, age 14
Springfield, Missouri

An exciting intergalactic adventure! In the distant future, a courageous warrior defends a kingdom from a dragon from outer space. Astounding sepia illustrations.
Printed Duotone
ISBN 0-933849-23-0

by Bonnie-Alise Leggat, age 8
Culpeper, Virginia

Amy J. Kendrick wants to play football, but her mother wants her to become a ballerina. Their clash of wills creates hilarious situations. Clever, delightful illustrations.
Printed Full Color
ISBN 0-933849-39-7

by Lisa Kirsten Butenhoff, age 13
Woodbury, Minnesota

The people of a Russian village face the winter without warm clothes or enough food. Then their lives are improved by a young girl's gifts. A tender story with lovely illustrations.
Printed Full Color
ISBN 0-933849-40-0

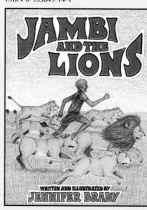

by Jennifer Brady, age 17
Columbia, Missouri

When poachers capture a pride of lions, a native boy tries to free the animals. A skillfully told story. Glowing illustrations illuminate this African adventure.
Printed Full Color
ISBN 0-933849-41-9

They Will Want to Read and Enjoy All of Them! **ORDER NOW!**

Jayna Miller
age 19

Lauren Peters
age 7

Michael Cain
age 11

Heidi Salter
age 19

Amity Gaige
age 16

Dennis Vollmer
age 6

Lisa Gross
age 12

Stacy Chbosky
age 14

Karen Kerber
age 12

David McAdoo
age 14

THE WINNERS OF THE 1992 NATIONAL WRITTEN & ILLUSTRATED BY... AWARDS FOR STUDENTS

FIRST PLACE
6–9 Age Category
Benjamin Kendall
age 7
State College, Pennsylvania

FIRST PLACE
10–13 Age Category
Steven Shepard
age 13
Great Falls, Virginia

FIRST PLACE
14–19 Age Category
Travis Williams
age 16
Sardis, B.C., Canada

GOLD AWARD
Publisher's Selection
Dubravka Kolanovic'
age 18
Savannah, Georgia

GOLD AWARD
Publisher's Selection
Amy Jones
age 17
Shirley, Arkansas

 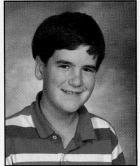  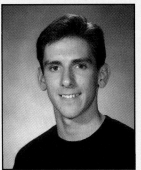 

ALIEN INVASIONS

When Ben puts on a new super-hero costume, he starts seeing Aliens who are from outer space. His attempts to stop the pesky invaders provide loads of laughs. The colorful illustrations add to the fun!

29 Pages, Full Color
ISBN 0-933849-42-7

FOGBOUND

A gripping thriller! When a boy rows his boat to an island to retrieve a stolen knife, he must face threatening fog, treacherous currents, and a sinister lobsterman. Outstanding illustrations!

29 Pages, Two-Color
ISBN 0-933849-43-5

CHANGES

A chilling mystery! When a teen-age boy discovers his classmates are missing, he becomes entrapped in a web of conflicting stories, false alibis, and frightening changes. Dramatic drawings!

29 Pages, Two-Color
ISBN 0-933849-44-3

A SPECIAL DAY

Ivan enjoys a wonderful day in the country with his grandparents, a dog, a cat, and a delightful bear that is *always* hungry. Cleverly written, brilliantly illustrated! Little kids will love this book!

29 Pages, Full Color
ISBN 0-933849-45-1

ABRACADABRA

A whirlwind adventure! An enchanted unicorn helps a young girl rescue her eccentric aunt from the evil Sultan of Zabar. A charming story, with lovely illustrations that add a magical glow!

29 Pages, Full Color
ISBN 0-933849-46-X

BOOKS FOR STUDENTS BY STUDENTS!®

Written & Illustrated by...
by David Melton

This highly acclaimed teacher's manual offers classroom-proven, step-by-step instructions in all aspects of teaching students how to write, illustrate, assemble, and bind original books. Loaded with information and positive approaches that really work. Contains lesson plans, more than 200 illustrations, and suggested adaptations for use at all grade levels — K through college.

The results are dazzling!
Children's Book Review Service, Inc.

WRITTEN & ILLUSTRATED BY... provides a current of enthusiasm, positive thinking and faith in the creative spirit of children. David Melton has the heart of a teacher.
THE READING TEACHER

...an exceptional book! Just browsing through it stimulates excitement for writing.
Joyce E. Juntune, Executive Director
The National Association for Creativity

A "how to" book that really works.
Judy O'Brien, Teacher

a revolutionary two-brain approach for teaching students how to write and illustrate amazing books

David Melton

Softcover, 96 Pages
ISBN 0-933849-00-1

LANDMARK EDITIONS, INC.
P.O. BOX 4469 • KANSAS CITY, MISSOURI 64127 • (816) 241-4919